The Giver

I0614946

Grades 7-8

Written by Michelle Lantaigne-Richard
Illustrated by Ric Ward

ISBN 1-55035-616-X
Copyright 1999
Revised February 2006
All Rights Reserved * Printed in Canada

Published in the United States by:
On the Mark Press
3909 Witmer Road PMB 175
Niagara Falls, New York
14305
www.onthemarkpress.com

Published in Canada by:
S&S Learning Materials
15 Dairy Avenue
Napanee, Ontario
K7R 1M4
www.sslearning.com

At  Glance™

Learning Expectations	Teacher Guide	Pre-Reading Activities	Reading Activities	Post Reading Activities
Understanding Concepts				
• Describe the characteristics of a story			•	•
• Interpret the meaning of the story			•	•
• State opinions and support ideas with proof from the text			•	•
• Develop comprehension skills	•	•	•	•
• Work cooperatively within a group and contribute in a meaningful way		•	•	•
• Listen and follow directions	•	•	•	•
Critical Analysis & Appreciation				
• Describe story elements			•	•
• Answer questions completely with supported proof from the story			•	•
• Identify conflict and resolution in a story			•	•
• Identify and state the point of view and motivation of each character			•	•
• Use research skills to locate information				•
• Compare and evaluate characters		•	•	•
Communication				
• Communicate and express ideas clearly in written form	•	•	•	•
• Express ideas in a variety of written forms (journal, poetry)	•	•		•
• Organize ideas effectively		•	•	•
• Express and support ideas and opinions verbally (debating)				•
• Usage of good vocabulary		•	•	•

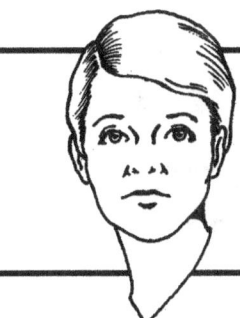

The Giver
by Lois Lowry

Table of Contents

The Giver
by Lois Lowry

The Giver
by Lois Lowry

Overall Expectations

The students will:

- become acquainted with the writings of Lois Lowry.
- be introduced to a society that is opposite to their own.
- reflect on societal differences and similarities.
- reinforce reading comprehension skills in a variety of assignments and activities.
- appreciate living in a free and democratic society.

Author Biography

Lois Lowry was born in 1937 in Honolulu, Hawaii. She graduated from both Boston University and the University of Southern Maine. Lois writes from her inviting, warm, small studio apartment in Boston whose walls are lined with books and photographs. Lois considers herself a visual writer who creates very vivid images while writing and reading. One of the most exciting features of writing, according to Lois, is that the reader is free to create his/her own visual world.

Many of her novels have developed from her own experiences and imagination. One of her first novels, A Summer to Die stemmed from a personal tragedy. Ideas for The Giver developed when she was visiting her aging father and came across a photograph of her sister who had died of cancer at a young age. Her father's memory was failing and he had forgotten about the tragedy. Out of this experience came an idea: What would it be like if we could repress bad memories and avoid the pains of our humanity? This experience became the basis for the novel The Giver.

Lois enjoys the writing process and utilizes a computer for her rough drafts. She marvels in the fact that the ideas just come out of her head and into the computer. When discussing the writing process, she explains that she completes many rewrites before printing out the first hard copy. She then proofreads her work and begins the next phase of rewriting. Lois feels that there is always something to write about, and she is never bothered by writer's block. Her creative energy is renewed when responding to the many letters from kids.

As a young person Lois considered herself shy, quiet and introspective. She derived satisfaction from the poems and stories she wrote. Today, when questioned about why she chose an adolescent audience for her work, she simply states that a book can be a vehicle for someone experiencing the sometimes lonely, and alienating experience of growing up.

The Giver

by Lois Lowry

Other Titles by Lois Lowry

A Summer To Die (1977) *Children's Book Award*

Find a Stranger Say Goodbye (1978)

Anastasia Krupnik (1979)

The One Hundredth Thing About Caroline (1985)

Anastasia and Her Chosen Career (1987)

All About Sam (1989)

Number the Stars (1987) *Newbery Award Medal*

Synopsis

Jonas, an insightful twelve year old, and his family reside in a unique society where there is no poverty, hate, fear, pollution, dissension, conflict, pain or love. To achieve this end the society has gained control over every aspect of their lives. Members of this society are not free to choose their career, spouse, home, number of children in the family unit, government and rules. The society attempts to achieve a lack of individuality and has successfully eradicated feelings from people's experiences generations ago. Feelings were thought to interfere with an individual's decision making process and now members of this community simply follow prescribed rules.

Jonas' mother works for the "Department of Justice" and his father was a "Nurturer" who cares for the newborns. All family units have one male and one female child. Jonas is the eldest and has a sister named "Lily". An immature baby named "Gabe" is brought home from Jonas' father's workplace for extra nurturing. Jonas' family, like all of the families, follow very structured rituals, e.g., each evening the family sits to reflect and discuss the events of the day and in the morning the family discusses dreams.

This society performs special yearly ceremonies for children from the age of 1 to 12. Families receive their children at the "Ceremony of the Ones" where children are named and distributed; "Sevens" receive a front buttoned jacket (showing independence); "Eights" are to do volunteer service; "Nines" receive their bicycles; "Elevens" receive a calculator and the females are able to wear undergarments and long trousers. At the Ceremony of the "Twelves", individuals learn of their future occupation.

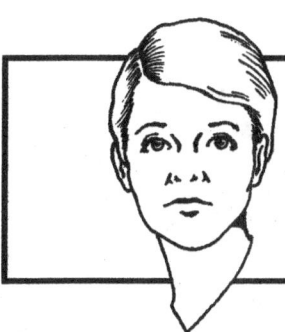

The Giver
by Lois Lowry

Jonas, a sensitive and bright boy is anxiously awaiting the Ceremony of the Twelves. Unbeknownst to him, he has been selected to be the "Receiver of Memories". This is a highly prestigious position and Jonas alone has been entrusted with this career. At one time everyone in this society was allowed to receive memories, but, unfortunately, this situation caused mass suffering and chaos. The elders had decided to restrict memories. Jonas is trained as the Receiver of Memory by the "Giver". His training is uncomfortable and treacherous. Memories are transferred from the "Giver" to Jonas and for the first time he experiences sunshine, color, books, cold, and sledding. After a while the "Giver" unloads more painful memories such as, war and death. Jonas begins to recognize that his society is deficient in many ways as he matures and seriously questions everything about his way of life.

Jonas learns about the release of Rosemary who had been chosen as a "Receiver of Memory" ten years earlier. After being exposed to poverty, hunger and terror she requested a "release" (death). The society granted her the release which affected the "Giver" very deeply. Jonas and the "Giver" plan for Jonas to escape form this community. However, if Jonas does escape to Elsewhere, the society will acquire the same knowledge of the past that Jonas received from the Giver. The Giver decides to remain behind when Jonas escapes to help the people cope with their newly acquired knowledge.

Jonas decides to leave ahead of schedule as he learns that the new baby, Gabriel, is scheduled for a release. Since Jonas is aware that release means killing, he is unwilling to let Gabriel die. He rescues the baby and flees from his family and his community at night. Over the course of a few days he experiences rain, snow, and the fragrance of flowers. An exhausted Jonas sees bright lights and hears singing and he believes he has arrived in Elsewhere with Gabriel.

The Newbery Medal

Since 1933 the Children's Services Division of the American Library Association has been presenting the Newbery Medal to an author for the most distinguished contribution to American literature for children. The award was donated by the late Frederic G. Melcher and named in honor of John Newbery (1713-1767). John Newbery was a famous eighteenth-century British bookseller and publisher of children's books. He was the first to publish children's literature and he encouraged original and creative work in this area. The Newbery medal is awarded to an American citizen or resident who has published during the preceding year. The recipient of the Newbery Medal receives a medal donated by the Melcher family. The Newbery Honor award and the Newbery Medal are prestigious awards which have come to denote the best in children's literature.

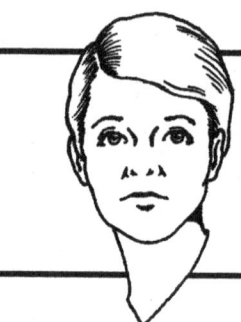

The Giver
by Lois Lowry

Newbery Medal Winners

1997	**View from Saturday**	E. L. Konigsburg
1996	**Midwife's Apprentice**	Karen Cushman
1995	**Walk Two Moons**	Sharon Creech
1994	**Giver**	Lois Lowry
1993	**Missing May**	Cynthia Ryland
1992	**Shiloh**	Phyllis Reynolds
1991	**Maniac Magee**	Jerry Spinelli
1990	**Number the Stars**	Lois Lowry

The Science Fiction Genre

Science fiction creates a future world with imaginary characters. These stories frequently deal with today's issues and problems in futuristic settings. Writers of science fiction often speculate on the potential uses of science and the potential future of humankind within this world and the universe. Along with speculation, the authors of this genre also like to declare an important statement or thesis. For example, a story may state facts about science, human nature, humans in relation to the universe, humans in conflict with the universe, or humans changing the human condition from which a thesis may be drawn.

Science fiction is a very significant genre as it tends to be very philosophical, intellectual and religious because it is concerned about the place of humans within the universe, ultimate destiny and the survival of humanity. Science fiction has been labeled the inquisitive fiction because it addresses such questions as: What if....?; If only...?; What if this goes on...?; and How can this be...?

Listed on the following page are some sub-themes of the science fiction genre with an example of either a film or a novel. (Generate other examples for each of these sub-themes).

The Giver
by Lois Lowry

Sub Theme	Author, Novel, Film Example
Space travel	Clarke, Arthur. 2001: A Space Odyssey
Superman	"Robocop"
Time travel and time warp	L'Engle, Madeline. A Wrinkle in Time L'Engle, Madeline. A Wind in the Door
Lost worlds	"Jurassic Park: The Lost World"
Social criticism	Baker, Robert. Brave New World. Orwell, George. 1984
Apocalypse	O'Brien, Robert. Z for Zachariah
Dystopia/utopia	Lowry, Lois. The Giver
Science fantasy	Bradbury, Ray. The Martian Chronicles Hughes, Monica. Devil on my Back Wells, H.G. The War of the Worlds
Robots, androids	Lucas, George. "Star Wars"
Aliens	"X- Files"

Discussion Themes

Before reading the novel, The Giver, the themes listed below may generate pertinent ideas, thoughts and discussion.

Family:

- define the role of family in our society
- identify your role in your family
- identify the roles of other members of your family
- name family traditions, rituals
- describe your family history
- name rules created by your family
- what activities do you do with your family?

The Giver

by Lois Lowry

Societal Rules:

- name some safety rules followed by members of your society
- name some school or class rules
- why are rules and regulations created?
- name some rules or laws which need to be changed and explain

Ceremonies:

- name and describe some ceremonies celebrated in your society (e.g., graduation, marriage, funeral)
- name some religious ceremonies (e.g., Baptism, Bar Mitzvah)
- why are ceremonies important?
- describe preparation for these events

Euthanasia:

- what is euthanasia?
- how do you feel about euthanasia?
- are there any circumstances when euthanasia is acceptable? (e.g., fatal illness, comatose patient)
- do people have a right to die?
- how do governments decide who should or should not die?

Genetic Engineering:

- how do you feel about selective breeding of human beings?
- should women be made to have their own babies- why or why not?
- what are the advantages and disadvantages of a society where people are created to suit the needs of the society?

Freedom:

- what are you free (and not free) to do?
- why is freedom a valuable commodity?
- what would it be like if you were given a career, a spouse and a family?
- are we ever totally free?

The Giver
by Lois Lowry

Introductory Activity: Brainstorming

Give small groups of students a large sheet of paper and some colored markers. Each member of the group should write a word, draw a picture or create a symbol to answer the following questions about the title of Lois Lowry's novel – The Giver.

What is worth giving to one another?

What is worth sharing with our families, friends, classmates, and other members of our society?

Sharing Ideas:

1. Have the small groups rotate to each of the other groups' sheets of paper. Students should read what is already on the paper and then record their word, picture or symbol.

or

2. Have small groups of students share by explaining their words, pictures or symbols to the whole group.

or

3. Give each person a number in the original group. Once the groups are finished recording on the original sheet, they can gather with similarly numbered students. In the new groupings, each student can place their symbol from the original sheet onto a new sheet. (These new groupings should generate a lot of discussion and curiosity).

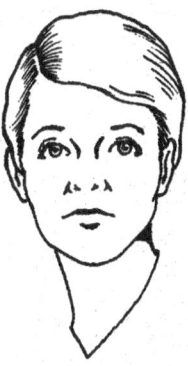

The Giver
by Lois Lowry

Introductory Activity: Creative Writing

Before reading the first few chapters of the novel <u>The Giver</u> use the following words or phrases in a short creative story. The words may be incorporated into your story in any order. Underline the words as they are used. The words or phrases have been taken from chapter one.

or

With a partner create a short story using the following words or phrases taken from chapter one.

or

Cut out the following words or phrases and have a small group of students put together a short oral passage.

Proofread your work and pay special attention to the verb tenses, spelling, sentence structure, paragraph structure, and voice.

1. Frightened meant that deep, sickening feeling of something terrible about to happen.
2. ...all citizens had been ordered to go into the nearest building...
3. Jonas was careful about language.
4. ...smiled at the recollection...
5. I felt so angry at him.
6. visitors
7. ...he felt strange and stupid...
8. sympathetically
9. ...look innocent...
10. The ritual continued.
11. future
12. ...this talk will be a private one...

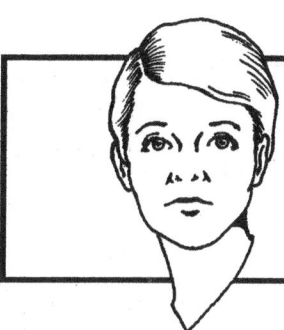

The Giver
by Lois Lowry

Response Journal and Discussion Circles

A **Response Journal** is an effective method for students to interact on a personal level with a novel. Students may use one of the three methods to complete a response journal. The purpose of the **response journal** is for students to write about their inner thoughts, feelings, reactions, questions, and to encourage students to make connections with the characters, setting, and plot.

Response journals may be shared with a partner, small discussion group or an entire class.

First Strategy – Open Ended:

Students may summarize one or more chapters in their own words. After each summary the student is responsible for creating a reflection or response about the assigned chapter(s). A set of guideline questions may be used to encourage varied responses (see sample).

Second Strategy:

Students may use the reflection sheet entitled, " Reflection on Societal Differences and Similarities" (p. 16) to make comments about the differences between Jonas' society and their own while reading the novel. Encourage students to reflect about "why" this society has opted for this new value system. Students should be able to depict feelings about these ideas such as, the elimination of choices, e.g., your career, spouse and family are selected for you.

Third Strategy – General Response Sheet:

Students may complete the sheet "Reading Response Journal" (p. 15) for one or more chapters in their own words.

Discussion circles are a time when responses are shared in small groups. People in a discussion circle are invited to ask one another questions or to make positive comments about the shared responses. Following "discussion circle" students may be invited to comment further or to pose questions about their own response or that of another student. Discussion circles should promote reflective inquiry on the part of the learner.

The Giver
by Lois Lowry

Ideas for Open Ended Response Journals

Character:

1. Name the characters in the chapter(s).
2. Identify what you liked or disliked about the character(s). Explain.
3. Describe the physical and emotional attributes of the character.
4. How did the character(s) interact with others? Describe any interpersonal conflict.
5. List questions you would like to pose to the character(s).
6. Can you empathize with the character(s) in any of the situations from this chapter(s)? Explain.
7. Explain how the character is changing?
8. Is the character believable? Why or why not?

Setting:

1. Describe the setting (time and place) in this chapter(s).
2. How is the setting important to this chapter(s)?
3. Draw a diagram to explain a particular setting from this chapter(s).

Conflict, Theme and Mood:

1. What did the author want you to feel or understand during this chapter(s)?
2. What is the theme of this chapter(s)?
3. Describe the conflict experienced in this chapter(s).
4. Explain the general mood of the chapter(s).
5. How do you feel about this chapter(s)? Explain.
6. What is the climax of this chapter(s)?

Writing Style:

1. Create a name for the chapter(s) and explain why you selected it.
2. Make a prediction about upcoming events.
3. Did the author use effective verbs and adjectives in this chapter(s)? Identify some examples.
4. Can you identify figurative language used in the chapter such as, similes?
5. Describe the pace of this chapter(s).

Reading Response Journal

Name: _____   **Chapter(s):** _____

Re-explain Describe the characters' attributes and actions. Describe the main events of the chapter(s). Explain the setting.	
Response Reflect on the chapter(s): **a)** How do you feel about the characters, society after reading? **b)** What do you believe is the theme? **c)** What questions would you pose to the characters? **d)** How is this chapter(s) important to the novel? **e)** Make predictions. **f)** Does it remind you of something perhaps from a film, video, book, etc...? **g)** Would you change anything about the chapter?	

The Giver
by Lois Lowry

Name: _____

Reflection on Societal Differences and Similarities

While reading the novel <u>The Giver</u> you will notice distinct differences between its society and your own. Record these differences/similarities and describe how you feel about them in the final column. Be sure to think about "Why" Jonas' society evolved its practices and values.

Jonas' Society	My Society	Reflection

The Giver
by Lois Lowry

Chapters One to Six

Vocabulary:

distraught	apprehensive	ironic	jeering
beckoning	aptitude	affectionately	chastise
rarity	reluctantly	droning	nondescript
tabulated	gravitating	hasten	rehabilitation
recounted	infraction	fidgeted	interdependence
prodded	indulgently	reprieve	relinquish
exuberant	meticulously	scrupulously	

Comprehension:

1. From whose point of view is the story told?
2. Describe how Jonas' society varies from your own.
3. What does being "released" from the community mean?
4. Explain how language is used in this community.
5. Give an example of Asher's character.
6. Identify the members of Jonas' family and explain their positions in the society.
7. What is the importance of the family rituals of "dreamtelling" and "sharing feelings"?
8. Name some societal rules.
9. Which rules does Jonas' father disobey?
10. What are the ceremonies? Describe the Ceremony of the Ones, Sevens, Eights, Nines, Tens, Elevens, Twelves and the Matching of the Spouses.
11. How does this society react to eye color?
12. What is a Birthmother? Why does Lily wish to be one?
13. Why was an announcement made to all male Elevens?
14. Why was Jonas intrigued by the apple?
15. What do you know about color in this society?
16. Why did children have to report "the stirrings" to an adult?
17. What is "Elsewhere"?
18. What is the difference between loss and release?
19. Why do the children in this society put in volunteer hours?
20. Who makes the important decisions in this society?

The Giver
by Lois Lowry

Chapters Seven to Twelve

Vocabulary:

exasperated	profound	retroactive	crescendo
benign	jaunty	indolence	compel
prohibition	requisitioned	integral	tentatively
deftly	obsolete	conveyance	fretful
admonition	exhilarating		

Comprehension:

1. Each person at the Ceremony has a number. What does it designate?

2. Why was Jonas upset during the Ceremony of the Twelves?

3. Name the assignment that the elders selected for Jonas.

4. Identify the qualities needed for Jonas' assignment.

5. What did Jonas' parents explain to him about a former Receiver?

6. Name the eighth rule which Jonas was to follow. Why did this bother him?

7. How was the Giver's home different than other family dwellings?

8. Why was the Giver eager to train Jonas?

9. Describe how the Giver transmitted memories.

10. What was the first memory which was given to Jonas?

11. What does Jonas learn about climate control?

12. What else did Jonas experience on his first encounter with the Giver?

13. Why doesn't Jonas share his first experiences in his new training with his groupmates?

14. What was his friend Fiona's experience of her first day of training?

15. What is Jonas experiencing in the apple, the sled and Fiona's hair?

16. What does Jonas learn about all of the colors? When was color lost?

The Giver
by Lois Lowry

Chapters Thirteen to Eighteen

Vocabulary:

alien	sinuous	indifferently	exempted
electrode	invigorating	daub	anguish
assuage	excruciating	ominous	placidly
serene	contorted	ecstatic	pervaded
luxuriating	permeated	realm	strewn
dejected	ruefully	luminous	carnage

Comprehension:

1. Why did this society remove choice making?

2. What happens to parents when their children are fully grown?

3. What is the role of the Giver in this society?

4. Describe a painful memory transmitted by the Giver to Jonas.

5. What was Jonas to gain by being the holder of memories?

6. How did Jonas comfort Gabriel?

7. Why did the Giver say, "Forgive Me"?

8. After the memory of war, the Giver shares happier memories with Jonas. What were they?

9. How does Jonas learn about the new concept of love?

10. What was Jonas' concern with the concept of love?

11. Why did Jonas stop taking his pills?

12. Which child's game upset Jonas?

13. Who was Rosemary and what was her fate?

14. What happened to the people when Rosemary was released?

15. Jonas was discussing the possibility of his disappearance with the Giver. Was the Giver upset by this discussion? Why or why not?

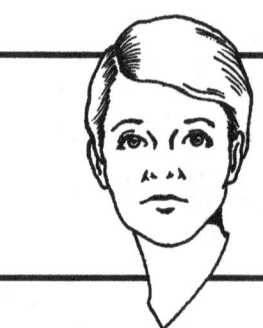

The Giver
by Lois Lowry

Chapters Nineteen to Twenty-Three

Vocabulary:

rueful	inconsiderate	unison	languid
fugitives	augmented	vigilant	haphazard
tentatively	diminished	wincing	relentless
meager	methodically	flagging	tantalizing
imperceptibly	lethargy	resignation	impeded
treacherously	incision	stealthily	emphatically

Comprehension:

1. What did Jonas view in chapter 19 which was very upsetting? Describe his reaction.

2. Why did the Giver explain Rosemary's release to Jonas? Who was she?

3. Why didn't Jonas want to go home? What was the Giver's response?

4. What did Jonas learn about what happens to the Old?

5. Jonas and the Giver devise a plan to change the current society. Describe it.

6. Why won't the Giver escape with Jonas?

7. What does Jonas learn about Gabriel before his escape and what is his decision?

8. Describe Jonas' experiences while riding away from his community.

9. How was the landscape different on Jonas' route?

10. Of what was Jonas most afraid?

11. How had the weather changed and how had Jonas reacted to his situation?

12. What weather condition had made his ride difficult?

13. Why did Jonas begin to feel happier at this difficult time?

14. How did he finally get to Elsewhere?

15. What did Jonas hear as he entered Elsewhere?

The Giver
by Lois Lowry

Vocabulary Ideas

1. Identify the meaning of each word.

2. Identify the part of speech for each word.

3. Use each word in a sentence.

4. Create a wordsearch.

5. Make flash cards for each of the new words. Use cards for a spelling bee.

6. Alphabetize the word list.

7. Identify words with prefixes or suffixes and underline the root words.

8. Create a paragraph and use as many vocabulary words as possible. Underline the words used.

9. Use a thesaurus to find synonyms and antonyms for the words.

10. Create an art piece and "hide" your vocabulary words within.

11. Make a chart of all of the characters and place appropriate vocabulary words in the proper section of your chart.

The Giver
by Lois Lowry

Quotes for Reflection

Review each of these quotations from the novel The Giver and describe what they mean and how they make you feel.

1. "...each such error reflected negatively on his parents' guidance and infringed on the communities sense of order and success." (Chapter Six)

    _____
    _____
    _____
    _____

2. "The punishment used for small children was a regulated system of smacks with the discipline wand: a thin, flexible weapon that stung painfully when it was wielded." (Chapter Seven)

    _____
    _____
    _____
    _____

3. "A name designated Not-to-Be-Spoken indicated the highest degree of disgrace." (Chapter Nine)

    _____
    _____
    _____
    _____

4. "It was extremely rude for one citizen to touch another outside of family units." (Chapter Thirteen)

    _____
    _____
    _____
    _____

The Giver
by Lois Lowry

5. "There was a time, actually – you'll see this in the memories later – when flesh was many different colors. That was before we went to Sameness. Today flesh is all the same..." (Chapter Twelve)

_____

_____

_____

_____

6. "We relinquished color when we relinquished sunshine and did away with differences... We gained control of many things. But we had to let go of others." (Chapter Twelve)

_____

_____

_____

_____

7. "Life here is so orderly, so predictable – so painless. It's what they've chosen." (Chapter Thirteen)

_____

_____

_____

_____

8. "...you used a very generalized word (love), so meaningless that it's become almost obsolete." (Chapter Thirteen)

_____

_____

_____

_____

9. "Memories are forever." (Chapter Eighteen)

_____

_____

_____

_____

The Giver

by Lois Lowry

10. "They know nothing... It's the life that was created for them. It's the same life that you would have, if you had not been chosen as my successor." (Chapter Twenty)

_____
_____
_____
_____

11. "The worst part of holding the memories is not the pain. It's the loneliness of it. Memories need to be shared." (Chapter Twenty)

_____
_____
_____
_____

12. "The community where his entire life had been lived lay behind him now, sleeping. At dawn, the orderly, disciplined life he had always known would continue again, without him. The life where nothing was ever unexpected. Or inconvenient. Or unusual. The life without color, pain, or past." (Chapter Twenty-One)

_____
_____
_____
_____

13. "If he (Jonas) had stayed, he would have starved in other ways. He would have lived a life hungry for feelings, for color, for love." (Chapter Twenty-two)

_____
_____
_____
_____

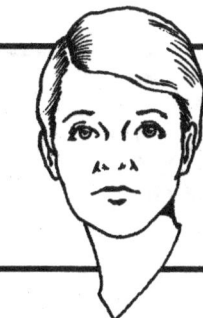

The Giver
by Lois Lowry

Looking at Grammar

Using grammar effectively is important in writing to assist the reader with determining meaning. Examine the example text from The Giver carefully. Identify the punctuation marks and explain why it was used in the chart below.

Example Text	Identify the Punctuaction	Explain why the Punctuation was used
"I don't know. they acted ...like..."	a) " " b) ...like...	
Two children – one male and one female – to each family unit.	a) -	
No one ever mentioned it; the disgrace was unspeakable.	a) ;	
"Well," she said, "I thought maybe just this once."	a) Well, b) she said,	
Dream-telling began with	a) -	

The Giver
by Lois Lowry

Lois Lowry's Writing Style

Authors consciously choose a specific style of writing that will best suit their story. They have many decisions to make such as:

- Which voice will best explain the story?
- Which verb tense will best enhance the story?
- Should I use figurative language, example: metaphors, similes...?
- What about the mechanics of the writing, example: punctuation, grammar?
- Which writing techniques should I include, example: foreshadowing, symbolism...?

Examine the Writing Style found in The Giver

Writing Technique	Find an Example from The Giver	Comment/Explanation
use of the dash -		
use of *italics*		
CAPITAL LETTERS		
hyphenated words		
vocabulary		
lack of metaphors and similes		
descriptive passages		
symbolism		

The Giver
by Lois Lowry

Exploring Writing Techniques

Writers make decisions when creating their novels. They need to effectively develop fundamental elements like setting, characters, theme, plot, and the sequencing of events. However, good authors also consciously decide to include writing tools like flashback, figurative language (metaphor, simile, personification, and repetition), symbolism, mood, foreshadowing, point of view, and characterization.

For each of the writing tools listed below, give an example from any source (example: film, novel, poem, script, television show, a speech, etc.). If applicable, use examples from The Giver.

1. **Flashback** – an interruption in the continuity of the story sends the reader/viewer to an earlier event

   Example: _____
   _____
   _____
   _____

2. **Figurative Language** – builds comparisons to assist reader/viewer to understand the characters, places or ideas
   – emblematic

   Example: _____
   _____
   _____
   _____

3. **Symbolism** – the use of an object to represent a feeling or an idea, example: dove symbolizes peace

   Example: _____
   _____
   _____
   _____

The Giver
by Lois Lowry

4. **Mood** – the feeling or atmosphere the reader/viewer gets from the story
   (example: peaceful, scary, disappointed)

Example: _____
_____
_____
_____

5. **Foreshadowing** – a clue in the story which indicates beforehand of things to come

Example: _____
_____
_____
_____

6. **Point of View** – the voice in the story
   – the first person point of view is told by the charter using "I"
   – third person point of view is told by someone other than the characters in the story using "she, he or they"

Example: _____
_____
_____
_____

7. **Characterization** – description of a character's physical and phychological attributes

Example: _____
_____
_____
_____

The Giver
by Lois Lowry

Discovering Themes

Novels are intricate pieces of writing which have more than one meaning. In fact, one should be cautioned against declaring the meaning of any novel because the meaning of a novel may be different from one reader to another. Each reader is a distinctive individual who will interpret and identify with certain themes found in the novel.

A central tendency woven throughout the novel is considered a theme. Lois Lowry has cleverly woven many themes throughout the novel <u>The Giver</u> Each of the various themes can be discussed separately but it is the total of all the themes which creates the meaning of the novel for the individual reader.

Discuss the themes listed as they relate to the novel:

1. Individuality – _____
   _____

2. Freedom – _____
   _____

3. The role of the family in society – _____
   _____

4. Rules within a society – _____
   _____

5. Euthanasia – _____
   _____

6. Genetic Engineering – _____
   _____

7. Special celebrations – _____
   _____

The Giver
by Lois Lowry

Characterization

The character in a novel is the central figure. Through his/her writing, the author can make a character respected, humorous, vile, loved, mischievous, despicable, or have any other characteristics that are necessary for the story. The author creates characters using many different approaches.

When the reader is describing a character every known detail must be taken into consideration so that the character's personality may be delineated. Once a character sketch is created, the essential points are gathered and then the reader may decide which characteristic is most suitable for the character (example: amiable, feared, etc.).

Developing Character Sketches and "Types"

Jonas:

1. Describe his physical attributes, example: age, appearance.
   _____

2. Describe what he likes to do.
   _____

3. Describe his attributes (character qualities, example: honest) and give an example from the text. (Look in Chapter Eight in particular.)
   _____

4. What "type" of character is Jonas?
   _____

The Giver:

1. Describe his physical characteristics.
   _____

2. Describe what he likes to do.
   _____

3. Describe his attributes and give examples from the text.
   _____

4. What "type" of character is The Giver?
   _____

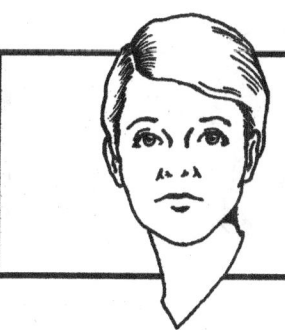

The Giver
by Lois Lowry

Developing Characterization

Read the passages taken from the text and answer the accompanying questions about characterization.

A) Taken from Chapter Nine.

"He had never, within his memory, been tempted to lie. Asher did not lie. Lily did not lie. His parents did not lie. No one did. Unless...

Now Jonas had a thought he had never had before. This new thought was frightening. What if others – adults – had upon becoming Twelves, received in their instructions the same terrifying sentence?

What if they had all been instructed: You may lie?

His mind reeled. Now empowered to ask questions of utmost rudeness – and promised answers – he could conceivably (though it was almost unimaginable), ask someone, some adult, his father perhaps: "Do you lie?"

But he would have no way of knowing if the answer he received was true."

1. What are Jonas' feelings about lying?

   _____

2. Why is Jonas feeling this way about lying?

   _____

3. Which words or phrases from the text help to demonstrate how Jonas is feeling?

   _____

4. Conceivably means: **possible**   **impossible**   **unimaginable**

5. Why are some of the words written in italics?

   _____

6. What does this passage indicate about this character?

   _____

The Giver

by Lois Lowry

B) Taken from Chapter Ten.

..."Beginning today, this moment, at least to me, you are the Receiver. "I have been the receiver for a long time. A very, very long time. You can see that, can't you?"

Jonas nodded. The man was wrinkled, and his eyes though piercing in their unusual lightness, seemed tired. The flesh around them was darkened into shadowed circles.

"I can see that you are very old." Jonas responded with respect. The old were always given the highest respect.

The man smiled. He touched the sagging flesh on his own face in amusement. "I am not actually as old as I look," he told Jonas. "This job has aged me. I know I look as if I should be scheduled for release very soon. But actually I have a good deal of time left.

"I was pleased, though, when you were selected. It took them a long time. The failure of the previous selection was ten years ago and my energy is starting to diminish. I need what strength I have remaining for your training. We have hard and painful work to do, you and I."

1. What evidence from the text suggests that the Receiver of Memory is physically old?

   _____

2. Select one word from the passage to show how Jonas responded to the older man.

   _____

3. Do you think that the former Receiver of Memory has a sense of humor? Why or why not?

   _____

4. How does the author describe the Giver's eyes? Is this a good description? Why or why not?

   _____

5. Why is the Receiver so welcoming to Jonas?

   _____

6. List two of the Giver's qualities.

   _____

The Giver
by Lois Lowry

Development of Revelation of Character

An author includes characters in his/her novel. Over the course of the novel sometimes the character undergoes significant changes. This is referred to as character development when fundamental changes occur in the character. Other times characters do not change but they are more fully exposed by the plot of the story. This is referred to as character revelation.

In order to analyze characters one should think about these question:

- How would you describe the character at the end of the novel?

- compare this description with a description of the character in the beginning of the novel.

- Decide whether or not the character has changed or is fully revealed through the actions of the story.

Complete the chart below for Jonas and the Giver.

	Jonas	The Giver
Character "Type"		
Character's Principal Actions		
Character's Principal Emotions and Attributes		
at the beginning of the novel		
at the end of the novel		
Development or Revelation? Explain.		

The Giver
by Lois Lowry

Considering Conflict

> **Conflict:** A problem in a story which needs to be resolved or worked on by the character(s).

Types of Conflict

1. **Character versus character:**		two characters have difficulty getting along
2. **Character versus society:**		a character at odds with a group of people
3. **Character versus nature:**		a character needs to contend with environmental problems
4. **Inner conflict or struggle:**		a character must deal with moral issues

Conflicts are included in a novel to bring the characters to life. Life, too, is a series of small conflicts interspersed with larger conflicts most of which need to be resolved. The resolution of the conflicts gives the novel it's story line. The more interesting and authentic the conflicts, the more believable the novel.

Minor conflicts may be resolved through a few pages or a chapter, however, other more serious or major conflicts may take the entire novel to unravel.

The Giver

by Lois Lowry

Complete the chart below.

Conflict	Example	Resolution
Character versus Character:		
Character versus Society:		
Character versus Nature:		
Inner Conflict:		

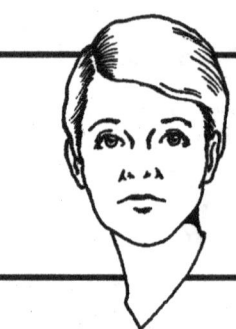

The Giver
by Lois Lowry

Working with Conflict

Identify three major conflicts and one minor conflict from the novel as a character versus character conflict; character versus society conflict; character versus nature conflict; or inner conflict. Tell why you believe it to be a minor or major conflict. How was the conflict resolved?

Explain the Example Conflict	Identify the Conflict	Major or Minor Conflict	Resolution

The Giver
by Lois Lowry

Thinking About Satire

> **Definition:** Satire is a literary work in which folly or evil in people's behavior is held up to ridicule. Satire is used to expose a vice.

Define the three words from the definition of satire and include their parts of speech.

Folly: _____

_____

Ridicule: _____

_____

Vice: _____

_____

Satirists can be shown to be really talking about their own world and critiquing through the fictional characters and their make believe activities. An example of a novel which is satirical is Lord of the Flies in which the school boys were stranded on a desert island. The boys create their own society and anarchy prevails. The author William Golden is critiquing and commenting on modern day society through the use of fictional characters and their experiences. He explores them as: fear, leadership, war and peace, primitivism, and the nature of society.

Using the above information, do you believe that Lois Lowry's novel The Giver could be classified as satirical? Or in other words, is the author really talking about our world and criticizing it through Jonas and the Giver? If so, explain. Think of some of the themes she examines.

_____

_____

_____

_____

_____

_____

_____

_____

_____

The Giver
by Lois Lowry

A Way With Words

Often times authors of science fiction will use unusual words or use words with an unconventional meaning in their work. Lois Lowry chose to put a twist on everyday English words. Translate each of the following words which appear in her novel.

New Society Term	Translation
dwelling	
caretaker	
sevens	
night clothes	
learning usages	
the evening of feelings	
comfort object	
newchild	
the house of the old	
birthmother	
nurturer	
food distribution	
bathing room	
stirrings	
groupmates	
sleeping room	
morning meal	
midday meal	
relief-of-pain	
unscheduled holiday	
midday meal out of doors	
wetness on his face	
evening meal	

The Giver
by Lois Lowry

Meteorology

Meteorology is the study of weather and weather patterns. The activities of humans are often controlled by the weather. For example, droughts play havoc for our agricultural areas; warm winters in the north disappoint skiers; and ice storms, mud slides, volcanoes, floods, tornadoes, hurricanes etc... destroy lives, and property. Lois Lowry recognized that humans are subjects of the weather and chose to do something about it in her novel, The Giver.

1. What do you consider to be the ideal weather? Explain.

   _____

   _____

2. How has weather affected your life (rain, snow, sleet, excess heat...)?

   _____

   _____

3. How did Lois Lowry control the weather in The Giver?

   _____

   _____

4. Write a descriptive paragraph outlining Jonas' reaction to the unusual weather he found in Elsewhere.

   _____

   _____

5. Gather newspaper articles or magazine stories about the impact weather has had on the world. Create a collage of headlines and images of devastating weather. Write a summary of the article. Be creative!

   _____

   _____

6. Research unusual weather: volcanoes, tornadoes, mud slides, floods, monsoons.

   _____

   _____

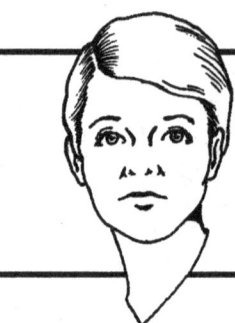

The Giver
by Lois Lowry

All in the Family

Compare and contrast your family, Jonas' family and a television family with whom you are familiar.

	Your Family	Jonas' Family	Television Family
List Traditions, Rules, Rituals			
How does the family spend time together?			
How are the various families similar to one another?			

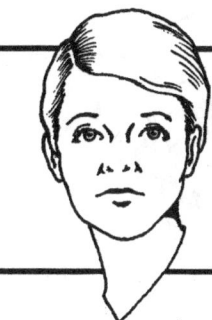

The Giver

by Lois Lowry

Careers

Identify each of the careers which were named in the novel and list characteristics necessary to engage in each career.

Word/Phrase	Name That Career	Characteristics
nurturer		
Department of Justice worker		
birthmother		
path-maintenance crews		
laborers		
food production		
planning committee		
collection crew		
chief elder		
fish hatchery attendant		
landscape workers		
instructor of the sixes		
director of recreation		
delivery crews		
caretaker of the old		
receiver of memory		

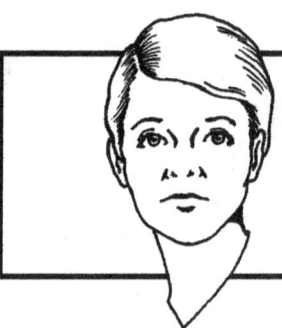

The Giver
by Lois Lowry

War Games

To Think About...

1. Describe some "war games" played by children in our society. Why do you think that young children engage in such play activities? Do you think that all war toys should be abolished? Why or why not?

2. Name some "violent" television shows or movies made for young children. Do you believe that the media has a responsibility to provide nonviolent and non-aggressive programs for our young people?

3. Watch the news to complete the following:
    a) record violent "hot spots" around the world where conflict is evident.
    b) list current violent crimes, e.g. murder cases, armed robbery

4. Do we have to live in such a violent world?

Action towards a nonviolent society:

1. Write a letter to a government official about your concerns.

2. With your friends, create nonviolent games for young people to play.

3. Prepare a speech about the importance of a nonviolent society.

4. Research famous peacemakers such as Mother Teresa, Martin Luther King, Ghandi, Bob Geldoff, etc...

5. Write a toy manufacturer urging them not to produce war toys.

6. Generate a way of dealing with conflict at all levels:
    a) personal conflict with others
    b) gang conflicts
    c) local political conflicts
    d) global conflicts

The Giver
by Lois Lowry

Family Memories

Draw or describe your cherished family memories in the boxes below.

Your favorite family memory	Your favorite family tradition or ritual
Your favorite family vacation or outing	**Your favorite family dinner**

What values do you see in family life? Do you think that Jonas' family had the same set of values? Why or why not?

The Giver
by Lois Lowry

Career Assignments

You are in charge of career assignments for five of your friends. Explain why you have made your selections. Use the career list found in this unit if necessary.

Name and Career Assigned	Reasons to Support your Decision

ELSEWHERE GAZETTE

Top story today: Jonas, 12, and his younger brother found abandoned in Elsewhere. Authorities indicated boys seem to be confused at this time.

Cold front to continue well into next week. Details inside

Humane society looking for good homes....

Starving, disoriented boys found abandoned near the outskirts of Elsewhere... Authorities stumped while looking for relatives.

"I was intrigued by the music that I heard as I slid down the hill into Elsewhere", stated Jonas.

Afterwords

"**Courage** looks you straight in the eye. She is not impressed with power trippers. Courage is not afraid to weep, and she is not afraid to pray, even when she is not sure who she is praying to. When she walks, she makes the journey from loneliness to solitude. The people who told me she was stern were not lying; they just forgot to mention she was kind."
~ J. Ruth Gendler

Top story continued from page 1...

Baby Gabriel is recouperating well at this time.

"The Giver helped plot my escape from my former dwelling", explains Jonas.

Jonas tries to explain the meaning of "release" to unbelieving authorities.

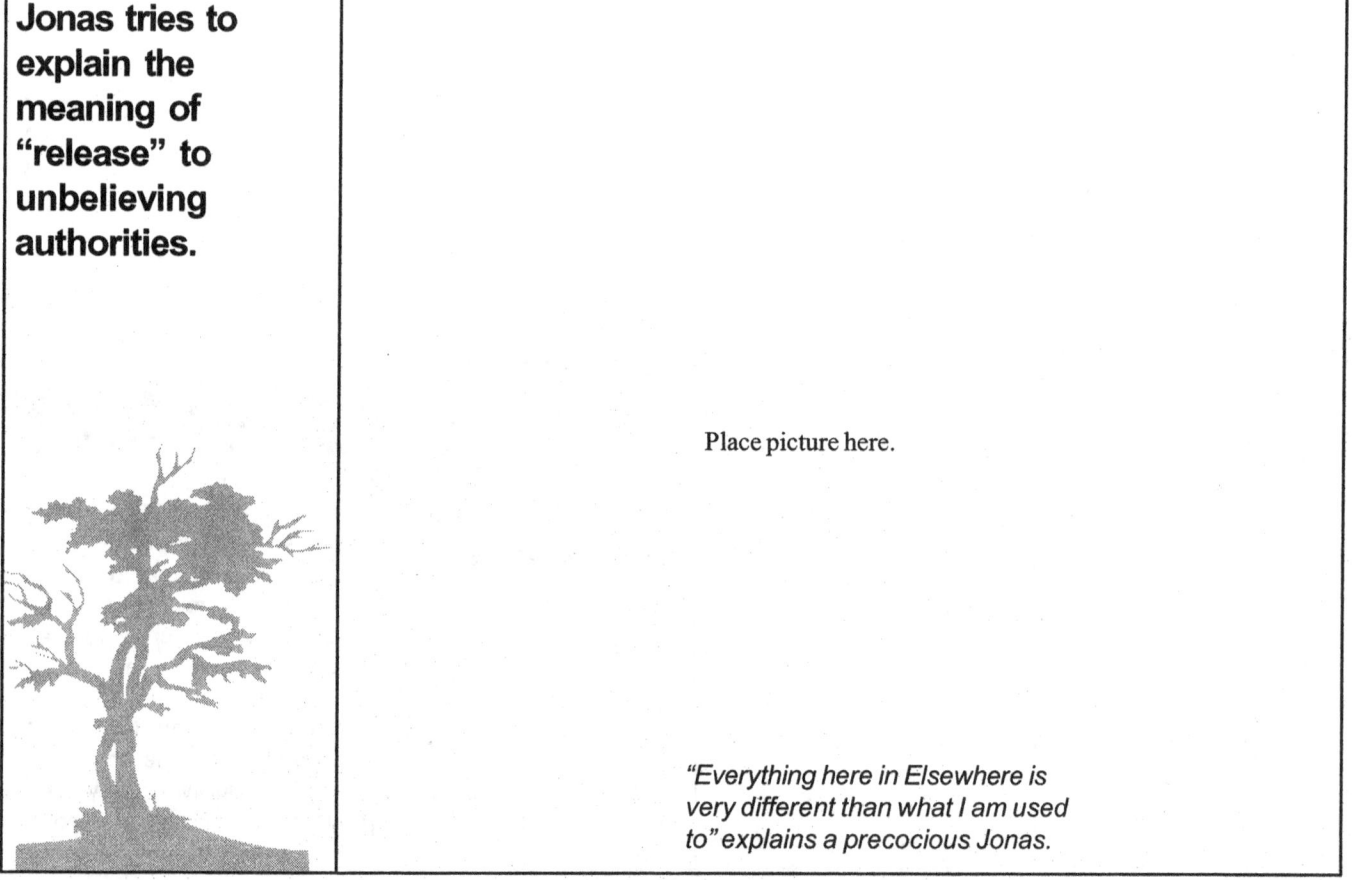

Place picture here.

"Everything here in Elsewhere is very different than what I am used to" explains a precocious Jonas.

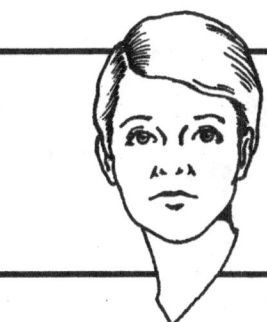

The Giver
by Lois Lowry

Love

1. Use a dictionary to define the word "**love**".

    In Jonas' society using appropriate language was essential. It was mentioned that the word **love** was overused.

    a) Do you agree that "love" is an overused word?

    _____

    b) What is the danger in overusing a word?

    _____

    c) Can you identify other overused words?

    _____

    d) Generate a list of songs which contain the word love.

    _____

Figurative Speech using the word "Love"

A **simile** is a comparison between two things using like or as.

> **Example: Love is like a golden sunrise.**

A **metaphor** is a comparison between two things without using like or as.

> **Example: Love is gently holding a baby..**

2. List as many similes and metaphors using the word "love".

    _____
    _____
    _____
    _____

3. Look through newspapers or magazines to find pictures and words associated with "**love**" to create a collage.

4. Create a free verse poem with love as your theme.

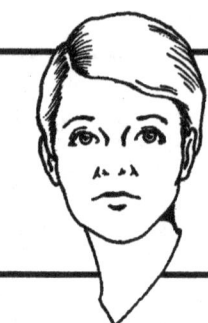
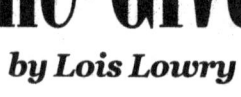

The Giver
by Lois Lowry

Rules were made to be broken?

List the rules given to Jonas as receiver of memory in the left hand column. In the right hand column explain why this was expected of Jonas.

Are any of these rules similar to your family or society rules? If so, explain. Which rules do you think are not appropriate.

Rules for Jonas	Expectations
1. Go immediately at the end of school hours each day to the Annex entrance behind the House of the Old and present yourself to the attendant.	

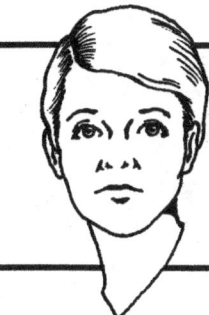

The Giver
by Lois Lowry

Rules, Rules, Rules

Compare and contrast the rules of Jonas' society with those of your own society.

Jonas' Society	Your Society
1. bragging	
2. mirrors	
3. taking items from others (e.g., Recreation Center)	
4. late for classes	
5. public humiliation (e.g., a reminder to male Elevens that objects are not to be removed from the recreation area)	
6. aircraft flying over community	
7. family structure (one male child and one female child)	
8. three transgressions and person is released	
9. application to get a child	
10. bicycle rules	
11. rude to touch others	
12. no citizen to leave dwelling at night unless on official business	
13. if you don't fit in you may apply for Elsewhere or release	
14. release	
15. nudity	

The Giver
by Lois Lowry

Volunteering

1. Children in the novel, <u>The Giver</u>, were expected to volunteer their time before the Ceremony of the twelves. This society felt that volunteering was an essential part of development. Why is it important to be a volunteer?

2. Where and how can young people volunteer their service in your community?

3. If you had to volunteer your time, where and how would you spend your time?

4. Find a volunteer (or create one) to interview about their position. Devise a list of questions before the interview.

Questions to Ask a Volunteer	Answers

The Giver
by Lois Lowry

Create a Video

1. With a partner pretend to be a videographer and interview Jonas in Elsewhere. Write a script of questions prior to taping the video and rehearse before taping.

2. Create a news report depicting the arrival of Jonas and Gabriel into Elsewhere.

3. Develop a short music video which details the music Jonas may have heard as he came to Elsewhere.

4. Make a video which explains Jonas' early life.

Travel Brochure

Create a three fold travel brochure for Elsewhere or Jonas' Society. Be sure to include pictures as well as information.

Group Memory Book

As a class, creatively construct a memory book. Each person could complete one page and then an editor could compile all of the pages to create a "Memory Book". Use photographs, pictures, anecdotes, poems, collages, etc...

Repetition as a Technique

Writers use many techniques to enhance writing such as, foreshadowing, figurative language, symbolism and repetition. Count the number of times the word **pain** is used in Chapter Fifteen. List the sentences the word **pain** appears in. Why was the word **pain** so significant during this story?

How is the technique of repetition useful?

Jonas' Elsewhere Journal

Pretend to be Jonas and create interesting journal entries for his first week in Elsewhere. Be sure to use all of your senses when describing the new sites and activities Jonas encountered.

The Giver
by Lois Lowry

Be an Anthropologist

Anthropology is the study of culture. Observations are noted and the differences between cultures can be analyzed. Anthropologists study language, work, ritual, activities, and family life. You are to pretend that you are an anthropologist who has secretly entered into Jonas' controlling society. You are expected to create a daily report for a week on your observations. Consider describing the following: "Ceremony of the twelves", a school day, morning ritual, a release, and transfer of memories.

Anthropological Log

Day One

Time: _____

Place: _____

Activity Observed: _____

Observations: _____

_____

_____

Day Two

Time: _____

Place: _____

Activity Observed: _____

Observations: _____

_____

_____

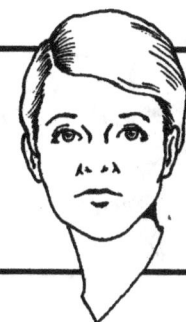
The Giver
by Lois Lowry

Day Three

Time: _____

Place: _____

Activity Observed: _____

Observations: _____

_____

_____

Day Four

Time: _____

Place: _____

Activity Observed: _____

Observations: _____

_____

_____

Day Five

Time: _____

Place: _____

Activity Observed: _____

Observations: _____

_____

_____

The Giver
by Lois Lowry

Debating Significant Issues

Academic Debating

1. Select issues from the novel which students may strongly agree or disagree with.

   a) euthanasia is appropriate
   b) the elderly should be released at the discretion of their care givers
   c) family members need to know everything about one another
   d) eliminating feelings from the society is a positive development
   e) controlling the weather is a great asset for a society
   f) sexual feelings must be suppressed
   g) a society where there is an aversion to love is beneficial

2. In groups of four, two students devise a position for and two students devise a negative position. Students must develop a position even if they do not agree.

3. Allow groups of two to consult with others who are working on the same position.

4. Students return to groups of two where they work on their final arguments.

5. Present final positions while opponents listen and record your arguments.

6. Debating begins.

Follow Up Activity:

Write a persuasive essay from these ideas.

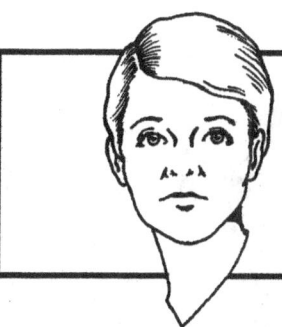

The Giver
by Lois Lowry

Persuasion – The Art of Arguing Intelligibly

Imagine that you have been selected by the mayor of your town to head a task force to study euthanasia in your community. Follow the plan below to create a strong argument to present to the mayor.

Task force Report on Euthanasia in my Community

1. **Introduction** – Clearly state our position on euthanasia.

2. **Background Information** – What laws exist in your area regarding euthanasia?

3. **Research** – Collect facts, statistics and information on euthanasia. Evidence must be based on current research on the topic. Be sure to consult many resources. You may wish to poll or interview people.

4. **Contradictory Ideas** – Anticipate contradictory arguments and plan to disprove them.

5. **Restate your position** – In your conclusion you should include a call for action which may be achieved by playing on the mayor's emotions.

The Giver
by Lois Lowry

Precise Language and Euphemism

Precise Language: Jonas' society encouraged precision in speech and thought. Asher's vocabulary choices were frequently corrected to emphasize accurateness in his speech. For example, when he was discussing why he was late for class he explained, "... I guess I just got distraught, watching them." The instructor suggested that the word "distraught" was too strong an adjective to describe his situation and felt that "distracted" was a more precise and appropriate word.

Euphemism: The definition of "euphemism" is a mild or vague expression substituted for a harsher or more direct one. For instance, people often use the expression she/he *passed away* when discussing someone's death. It seems that the euphemism "passed away" is less harsh than using the precise word. Although Jonas' society emphasized precise language they also used euphemisms. Identify some euphemisms and the corresponding precise word.

Euphemism	Precise Language
release for	
The Giver for	

After thinking about euphemisms why do you suppose that they are used? List some in the chart.

_____

_____

Euphemisms in our Society	Precise Language
restroom or washroom	

The Giver
by Lois Lowry

Black and White

Jonas and the Giver are part of a society which literally sees everything in black and white. The people within the society cannot see any color. Imagine living in the world and never seeing the range of color in nature – from the vividness of a sunset to the brilliance of a garden. It is estimated that one in twenty males and one in 100 females in our society are affected by color blindness whereby they are born without the ability to detect color. Investigate color blindness using the internet or other resource materials. Find its genetic cause.

Create a cartoon storyboard of a scene from the novel <u>The Giver</u> but do not use any color. Be sure to include precise language for the dialogue.

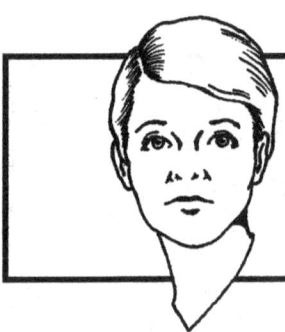

The Giver
by Lois Lowry

Media Literacy

Movie Producer's Dream

Imagine that you have been selected to produce <u>The Giver</u> for the big screen.

1. One of your first jobs is to select the cast. Identify actors who will play the leading and supporting roles. Explain your selection.

2. Select one scene from your movie to produce for a "trailer" to be shown in theaters around the world. Trailers are an effective form of advertising as the filmgoer gets to see a few minutes of actual footage from your film. To complete this task a lot of planning needs to be done prior to shooting. Here are some things to consider while you plan your film "trailer".

   a) Select the most appropriate scene you think will entice filmgoers to your movie and explain why.

   b) Prepare the actual script for the characters and use stage directions.

   c) Draw or describe the costumes the characters will wear.

   d) Choose a piece of music and/or sound effects to accompany your trailer.

   e) Discuss cinematic techniques that you will use:

   camera angle – high angle above subject; eye level or a flat shot or low angle below the subject.

   zoom in or zoom out on subject – *camera distance* – extreme close up, close-up, medium shot, long shot.

3. If it is possible to borrow a video camera, produce your trailer and present it to an audience. Ensure that the director and actors are fully aware of their roles and rehearse before filming.

4. Share your "trailer" with an audience and have them critique your work.

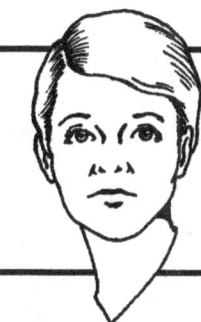

The Giver
by Lois Lowry

Web Site Development

Create a web site for the novel The Giver. Before you begin, plan your web site carefully by completing the outline below. Decide on a focus for your web site, for example educational or advertisement.

URL (Address)	www.
Title for the Home Page	
List the Links found on the Home Page (Site Map)	
Sketch Graphics found on the Home Page	
Text on the Home Page	
E-mail Response and/or Chat line for Reader Response	

Answer Key

Chapters One to Six: *(page 17)*

1. Jonas is an eleven-year-old boy.
2. Jonas' society has many rules for its members which encourage sameness, compliance, loyalty, conformity and order.
3. "Released" from the community means that the member is shunned by the community and is sent to Elsewhere or is punished in some form.
4. Language is extremely precise or members will suffer from public ridicule.
5. Asher is a friend of Jonas and is somewhat irresponsible, absent minded and careless. He doesn't seem to fit in. For example, he is consistently late for class.
6. Jonas' Mother works for the "Department of Justice", his Father works as a "Nurturer", his sister Lily is a Seven.
7. Families are to share intimate feelings with one another and converse about daily experiences.
8. There are many rules for the members of this society: each family was to have only two children, everyone does volunteer work, bike riding allowed at Nine, pills were taken for "Stirrings", refrain from use of the word release, after 3 transgressions members are released, objects not to be removed from the recreation area and citizens were not to leave their premises at night.
9. Jonas' father disobeys the bike riding rule and he named his charge - Gabe.
10. The ceremonies are an annual event where children are given new roles and activities until Twelve. Ones- are named and placed with a family; Sevens - receive jackets buttoned in the front; Eights - volunteer jobs assigned; Nines - able to ride bikes; Tens - females are able to wear hair short; Elevens - females given undergarments and all given a calculator; Twelves - assigned their role in the community; " Matching of the Spouses" - people may wait months or years to be assigned an appropriate spouse if matched at all.
11. Almost all citizens had dark eyes. Since the norm was to have dark eyes no one mentioned or called attention to those that did not. Jonas had lighter eyes.
12. A birthmother is a woman who gives birth to three babies and for the rest of her adult life she is a Laborer. Lily thought it would be wonderful to be a birthmother because they are pampered before giving birth. However, her mother told her that they never get to see their new children.
13. Jonas was being disciplined for taking an apple home through public humiliation.
14. The apple seemed to change on Jonas in mid air.
15. These people do not perceive a lot of color, rather they see shades.
16. Children had to report "Stirrings" (sexual feelings) so that they could be given a pill to repress sexual feelings.
17. Elsewhere is anywhere outside of this rigid society.
18. Release is the end of a person's life when they are very aged. Loss is the death of a child.
19. Volunteer hours are used to help children train for their future careers.
20. The elders make the decisions in this society.

Chapters Seven to Twelve: *(page 18)*

1. The number designated the chronological order in which the children were born.
2. Jonas' assignment was held until the last and he was concerned he would not receive an assignment.
3. Jonas was to be the Receiver of Memory.
4. Qualities include: intelligence, integrity and courage.
5. His parents told him that a previous Receiver failed and they never saw her again. Her name is not to be spoken nor passed on.
6. Jonas had a series of rules to follow and the eighth one was that he may lie. This upset his moral integrity.
7. His home was much like all other dwellings except that it held many books and carvings on the furniture.
8. The Giver felt weighted by all of the memories of this society and wanted to unload on Jonas.
9. The Giver lays his hands on Jonas' back and memories mysteriously flood into Jonas.
10. The first memory was of a sled ride.
11. Snow limits the growing season and with climate control agricultural productivity is increased. Hills interfere with traveling.
12. Sunshine and sunburn.
13. Jonas was cautioned not to tell about his training. Moreover, no one would understand his experiences.
14. Fiona had an exciting first day and realized that there was a lot to learn like administrative work, dietary rules and punishment for disobedience.
15. The color red.
16. He learns that colors add a vibrancy to the community that should be shared with others. Color was lost when the society relinquished sunshine and gave up differences.

Chapter Thirteen to Eighteen: *(page 19)*

1. People were being protected from the stress of decision making and the pain of making inaccurate decisions.
2. Parents with grown children do not live in the family unit but live with other Childless Couples.
3. To keep memories and to counsel the Elders when they are in need of memories to help resolve problems.
4. Jonas experienced breaking a leg which was terribly painful. War; and death of Rosemary.
5. Jonas would receive wisdom, feelings, love, color and emotions.
6. Jonas gave him a comforting memory of a sail on the clear lake.
7. The Giver shared with Jonas the meaning of war and realized how terrifying it must be.
8. Memories of a birthday party, museum, riding a horse and walking through the woods a campfire and a family at Christmas.
9. The Giver shares his favorite memory of a family gathering to teach Jonas about love.
10. Jonas felt that there was a risk involved with love but he wasn't sure how.
11. He wanted to start feeling everything including sexual urges.
12. Jonas was upset by a war game he and his friends were playing.
13. Rosemary was the former "Receiver of Memory" (the Giver's daughter) who requested a release because the pain was far too excruciating.
14. The people received the memories which had been transferred to Rosemary upon her release.

15. The Giver was not upset by the discussion about the loss of Jonas. He believed if Jonas was lost the Giver could assist the people to deal with the new memories caused by Jonas' disappearance.

Chapters Nineteen to Twenty-Three: *(page 20)*

1. Jonas viewed the release of the smaller twin performed by his father. Jonas carefully watched his father weigh the twins and decide which would be given a lethal injection. Jonas let out a loud shriek "He killed it! My father killed it!".
2. Jonas had a misperception about her release. He believed that Rosemary wasn't brave enough but the Giver explained that Rosemary asked to inject herself which showed incredible strength. Rosemary was the Giver's daughter.
3. He was appalled that his father killed an innocent baby. The Giver allowed him to stay overnight.
4. Jonas learns that the Old are killed when they are released.
5. Jonas is going to escape the community before the December Ceremony. Jonas will leave his home in the middle of the night and will hide in a storage area of the vehicle with food for his journey. When the Ceremonies begin everyone will be preoccupied. Later the searchers will find his clothes and bike by the river and believe him to be dead.
6. The Giver won't go with Jonas because he would like to help the people to deal with their feelings. The Giver remained committed to the Society.
7. Jonas learned that Gabriel had been scheduled for release so he decided to take Gabriel with him.
8. Jonas pedals during the night and soothes Gabriel by transmitting soothing memories to him. He slept during the day in a grove of trees. He was terrified of the search planes.
9. The landscape on Jonas' route had narrower roads which were unattended. There were lots of rocks and ruts in the road. Trees became more numerous, many streams were evident and they began to see wildlife such as, birds and flowers.
10. Jonas feared that they would starve. He began to fish, and pick berries, but they were still very hungry.
11. Jonas experienced two days of rain which made them cold, and wet. Jonas was now exhausted and weak from hunger which made him weep.
12. The heavy snows made his ride difficult.
13. Memories of joy flooded through him which strengthened him.
14. On a sled
15. Jonas heard music and people singing.

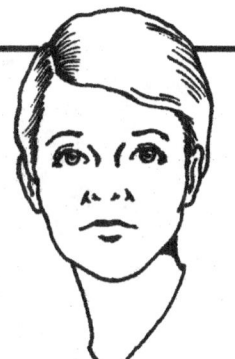 # The Giver
by Lois Lowry

_____
_____
_____
_____
_____
_____
_____
_____
_____
_____
_____
_____
_____
_____
_____
_____
_____
_____
_____
_____
_____
_____
_____
_____
_____
_____

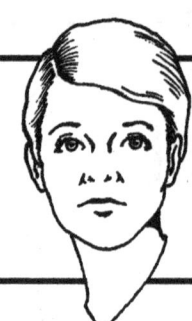

The Giver

by Lois Lowry